Rune of the Witch

Heather G. Harris

For my awesome supporters on Patreon, with special mention to Amanda Peterman, Melissa and Kassandra. I am so grateful and humbled by your belief in me.

Content Warnings

If you have any concerns about triggers, please see the full content warnings on Heather's website.

Please note that all of Heather's works are written in British English with British phrases, spellings and grammar being utilised throughout. If you think you have found a typo or another error, please do let Heather know by contacting her at heathergharrisauthor@gmail.com so it can be remedied. Thank you.

Chapter 1

If I were the sort of person who swore aloud, then this would be the man who would drag expletives from me. 'No,' I said firmly, turning back to my paperwork. 'Go away.'

Out of the corner of my eye I saw that the griffin stayed completely motionless and ignored my imperious command. His lion's body filled my office, the white feathers around his face and neck shone, but it was the eyes – and the claws – that were most dangerous. The eyes, because they missed nothing, and the claws because they could kill you before you blinked. There was a shimmer, and standing in front of me was a man who looked no less dangerous than he had in his griffin form moments before.

He had dark hair, olive skin and dark eyes. He was dressed in black combat trousers, black boots and a black T-shirt that might as well have been painted on. The shirt showed off hard, corded muscle. Human or not, he was still more deadly than your average viper – and I hate reptiles.

Bastion studied me like I was a puzzle he couldn't quite work out and then, in blatant contravention of my order, took the seat opposite me. He stretched out his legs, crossed his ankles and lounged back. Indolently. Bastard.

'I need your help,' he said calmly.

I looked up again. 'You need to go away,' I replied evenly. 'I don't have anything to say to you. Not now, not ever.'

He studied me. 'There are lives at stake, witch.'

'Not mine. Leave.'

His eyes narrowed; they were now so dark as to be almost black – as black as his soul.

'I want nothing to do with you.' There, that was clear enough. He still didn't move. 'Get out!'

He continued to ignore me as if I hadn't spoken. My blood started to simmer.

'Let me tell you a little about why I want your help. Then, if you still don't want to assist me, I'll leave willingly,' he offered.

'You'll leave *un*willingly,' I threatened through gritted teeth, reaching for the potion bomb in my jacket pocket.

'I wouldn't do that if I were you,' he said softly. The words carried on the air like the caress of a silk handkerchief with a sharp blade wrapped inside it. He was like a coiled spring. Suddenly violence was in the air. As quick as I am, one wrong move on my part and blood would be spilled...

I eased my hand away from the potion bomb. Suddenly my mouth was dry and, though I refused to admit it, fear had sent my heart careening. I glared up at him, hating this man who set my pulse racing like a rabbit being hunted.

'Fine,' I spat out. 'Tell me what you want and then you will *leave.*'

His lips turned up the barest amount. On another man, his expression might have been described as a smile but I knew he wasn't smiling because that would surely shatter his stony face. 'A griffin is missing,' he explained. 'She's been out of contact for two days.'

'So? Maybe she just doesn't want to talk to you,' I suggested snidely. I steadfastly ignored the tendril of concern for the missing woman which was worming its way into my thoughts. She wasn't my problem, dammit. I had a whole coven to look after.

My comment struck a chord. He stilled for a heartbeat, but it was long enough for me to note that I had scored a direct hit. He had also wondered if she simply didn't want to talk to him. There was a history there. Whoever she was, she was someone special to him. And I didn't care about that, *not at all.*

'You're not my first choice of investigative partner,' he admitted finally.

'No?' I said sarcastically. 'My heart is broken.'

He shrugged. 'Jessica Sharp wasn't available.'

Jessica Sharp, also known as Jinx, is a PI. She's probably one of my best – and only – friends, which shows the dire state of my life because I've known her only a handful of months. Jinx was unavailable because she was off somewhere on her honeymoon. At this moment, a tropical holiday sounded like a really good idea.

'I need you to scry for the griffin,' he continued.

I raised an eyebrow. 'You can't track her with all of your exceptional skills?' There was only a hint of sarcasm in my tone. As much as I hated him, I knew he was an excellent tracker and it was rare for him not to be able to find someone.

'No,' he said simply. 'I can't. And I have a tracking rune on her, so I should be able to find her anywhere in the world.'

I realised then that something else was riding him: anxiety. Well, well, well ... Bastion, the deadliest assassin in living memory, had a heart. Somewhere. 'Why would you track another griffin?' I asked, curiosity pulling me into the conversation despite myself.

I could see that he didn't want to answer me but he admitted grudgingly, 'She's my daughter, Charlize.'

'Poor girl.'

He glared. 'You can chuck many accusations my way – and many of them would be true – but being a shit father isn't one of them. I raised my daughter. I was there for every punch and kick, every martial arts grading and every knife-throwing competition. She knows I'm proud of her, despite the fact that she's made a few poor decisions recently. She's young. She'll learn.'

A hard shard of jealousy lanced through me. Ugh. Even Bastion had been a better father than mine.

My dad left mum and me when I was six, strolling out without so much as a 'ta-ta'. Mum was convinced he'd been kidnapped. She had tried to scry him without success, so she called in the big guns – the Connection. The Connection detectives did nothing; they confirmed he was alive and well and that he had left of his own volition. Case closed.

So Mum had hired a PI who found Dad within a week. Apparently, my dear father was living with another woman and three kids in a house runed up to the hilt so Mum and I couldn't find him. *We* were the extra family; Mum had been his bit on the side. I guess his other wife found out about us and gave him an ultimatum so he walked out on us and didn't look back. Neither did we. Screw him.

I met Bastion's eyes. 'I'll think about it. Now leave.' Much as I despised Bastion, I wanted to help his daughter. She couldn't help who her father was. I wanted to help her but I didn't want to help *him*. Unfortunately, if I did one then I did the other. Another witch could help him. Anyone that wasn't *me*.

Bastion's jaw tightened. 'She's in danger. I need your help now, not in three weeks. You've refused to help me and that's your prerogative, but she doesn't deserve to die for *my* sins.'

I noticed he didn't deny that *he* deserved to die for his sins.

I studied him for the first time since he'd sauntered into my office. Looking at him properly, I could see that the black witch's curse was taking its toll on him. His eyes were tired and underscored with bags, and I wondered if his strength was starting to fade.

I'm a lot of things. I'm a witch, I'm a bitch and yes, I'm petty as heck. But my grudge with Bastion wasn't petty; it was justified. And I was determined to see that he died for it.

Chapter 2

Bastion's visit had unsettled me more than I cared to admit and after half an hour I gave up on the paperwork as a bad job. Being coven mother gives you too much paperwork; I dreaded to think how much I would have to deal with if I managed to secure the position as the Symposium member for the witches.

There had been a power vacuum ever since the last Symposium member, Sky, was killed. The coven council was moving excruciatingly slowly in appointing the new member; in the meantime, members of the council took turns attending the Symposium meetings. I suspected that they liked the taste of extra power and weren't in a hurry to relinquish it.

The Symposium runs the Connection – the governing body for all supernatural beings that exist in the Other realm. I wanted to be on it – heck, I wanted to *rule* it – but one thing at a time. I wanted to craft the change that the Connection so desperately needed, and I wanted to do it from within. It was generally accepted that the next witch member would either be me or my rival, Kassandra Scholes. Kassandra was the mother to the Liverpool coven, which gave her the edge because Liverpool is where the coven council sits. She could schmooze them all whilst I was stuck heading the Home Counties coven.

I forced my hands to relax. I possessed skills that Kassandra didn't have, and I was still a strong contender despite the fact that I lacked my own familiar. I just needed to do something extraordinary to convince the council of my fitness to rule. And I'd be good at it, dammit. I'd be the best witch leader in history. If they gave me the chance, I wouldn't squander it.

Bastion's scent lingered in the air, spicy, with sandalwood and a distinctive maleness. His energy bothered me; it was dark and enticing. Something else lingered that I refused to admit, even to myself.

I pulled out a pre-rolled bundle of sage and lit it at one end before gently blowing out the flame and letting the embers linger. The tendrils of smoke drifted through my office, cleansing it of the day's traffic and the scent of *him*. Celts had been burning sage for centuries, and something about the smell always settled me.

I took in a steadying breath and tried to consider his request logically. Should I help him? It went against almost every instinct I had. I wanted to destroy Bastion like he had destroyed me, but I didn't believe in letting a child suffer for the sins of their parent – even though Charlize was hardly a child. I chewed the inside of my lip; I was conflicted and I knew that the wrong choice either way would have consequences which I'd have to live with. It would be so much easier if I didn't have a conscience – damn you, Jiminy Cricket.

I ground out the bundle of sage against the burning tray, extinguishing the delicate embers. Never leave a fire unattended. I wanted to ignore Bastion's request, to dismiss it out of hand, but a part of me – a very vocal part – didn't want to leave someone missing. I remembered the feeling of being lost and alone. I'd been kidnapped once and Lucy had come to find me. Lucy was the alpha werewolf of the local pack, and she was someone I could tentatively call my friend, though she was a very recent addition to the miniscule roster.

I needed counsel. That rarely happened, but it would have been foolish of me not to take advantage of the Crone's rare visit. She was travelling with the Maiden and the Mother, giving advice to witches up and down the UK. The triune usually toured the covens once every five years, but Sky's death had prompted this particular visit.

Sky had become a black witch. According to my sources, the coven council had commissioned the Crone to travel around the country to ferret out any other black witches who might be hiding amongst us. The triune's usual visits were a smokescreen to allow the Crone to dig deep into the local covens whilst the Maiden and the Mother held court.

I was gratified that the Crone had found not a hint of malpractice in my coven because I pride myself on running a tight ship. The Crone is one of the few people I truly admire; for many years she was a friend to my mother, Luna. I had always looked up to her; having her secure the position of Crone – a position for life – had only cemented my admiration.

Both the coven council and the Symposium member positions are jobs for a four-year period; after that you have to be re-elected and the longest you can serve is eight years. Crone is the only position in witching society that you hold for life. Maiden and Mother aren't similarly blessed because the Maiden has to be young and the Mother has to have recently birthed a child.

In the old days, covens lived together in villages, but now we have adapted our living practices to mimic modern life. The covens have their own apartment blocks. At the top of mine is a rarely used guest suite. I checked the time: 10pm. The Mother and the Maiden would be hosting an after-dinner gathering. My duties as coven mother made me waver for a moment. I *should* attend the circle now that I was free, but instead I jogged up the steps. I needed advice and I wasn't a fan of socialising; besides, my presence would put a dampener on the proceedings.

I knocked once on the door of the guest suite. I didn't want to disturb the Crone if she was sleeping, though if she'd kept the same habits she'd had when I was child I very much doubted she would be.

'Come in,' called a thin reedy voice.

I obeyed – rare for me. 'Crone,' I greeted her respectfully, one hand held to my heart.

'Coven Mother, be welcome.' She smiled warmly and my own lips turned up in response.

'Thank you.' Now that I was here, I wasn't sure what to say. I cleared my throat. 'I seek counsel, if I may. I've been approached by a griffin. He wishes to hire me to find his missing daughter.'

The Crone looked at me with her too-knowing eyes. 'Bastion. The runes shook when he arrived – though he did at least use the front door.' She sounded amused. 'Bastion asked for your help and you despise him.'

I stifled a grimace; I didn't realise our enmity was so widely known. 'He killed my—' lover? '—friend.'

There was so much meaning in that one word. Jake had been everything to me, my one true friend in the whole world, and I'd been forced to keep him hidden like a shameful secret. We believed that one day he would be free and we would be together properly, but Bastion had killed him before that day had come. Jake and I never got the future I'd dreamed of because of the griffin.

'He is a griffin,' she said gently. 'They must kill to survive. It is foolish to be angry at the clouds for raining because we all need water. In the same way, death is a part of life. Deaths are necessary to control the populace. Deaths at the hands of griffins are even more necessary, lest the griffins lose their fragile grip on their urges and slaughter all of us.'

She wasn't telling me anything I didn't already know and I suspect my resting-witch face said as much. I folded my arms. 'Regardless, I do not have to assist him,' I said grumpily.

'You do not.' She studied me, her brown eyes looking at me with a sympathy that made me grimace. I needed no one's pity.

Abigay had changed a lot in the last few years. Her dark afro had turned white in sharp contrast with her dark, lined skin, but her eyes were the same as was the warmth of her smile. Even at 10pm, her lips were painted with the same bright pink lipstick that I remembered from my childhood. It was enough to loosen my tongue.

'Aunt Abigay,' I started. She looked at me with a hint of censure; now that she was the Crone I wasn't her family to be gifted the use of her name. I continued anyway; she was family to me, what little I had. Her, Mum, Oscar – that was it. 'What should I do?' I entreated.

'You know the answer to that,' she said firmly before changing the topic. 'I visited your mother today. She was looking well.'

I refused to let the conversation digress. 'I don't want a moral compass; I want to know what the

Goddess advises. What should I do? Please – will you consult the stars for me?'

The Crone shook her head to deny me and my stomach lurched. She pressed her lips together at my poorly hidden dismay and gave a soft sigh. 'Very well. Come, child.'

'I'm forty-two,' I pointed out drily.

She smiled. 'You'll always be a child to me, with skinned knees and a guarded heart.'

That stung a little. If my heart is guarded, it is my father's fault. Nevertheless, Aunt Abigay is certainly in that beating organ.

She pushed herself upwards. 'Come then, princess, let's consult the stars.' The old nickname made me smile and let me know she'd forgiven me for using her name.

We left the apartment and took the stairs up to the roof. As I opened the door, the cool April air rushed inside. I helped Abigay over the last step and we made our way to the seats on the rooftop terrace. Darkness hung above us, pierced by glittering stars.

We weren't alone. I glared at the teenage couple who had undoubtedly been making out until they were so rudely interrupted. 'Ria, Henry, off to bed with you,' I ordered sharply. 'Separately,' I clarified.

Even in the darkness, I knew they were blushing. 'Yes, Coven Mother,' they chorused, slinking away and shutting the door behind them as they went. I frowned; it is dreadful to be a slave to hormones. I'd have to make sure the Mother or the Maiden had a quick chat with them about contraception.

Abigay snorted. 'You were young once. I caught you many a time snuggled up with Jake.' She winced straight after the name left her lips. 'Sorry.' She touched the top of my arm.

As far as she was aware, Jake had died when we were in our twenties, a victim of an acidic potion to the face. The truth was that I'd saved his life and hidden him away from his would-be assassins. The attack had done its work, though; Jake had been blinded and, for him, having to stay hidden was a long slow death. Jake was a sore topic, now and always.

'The stars,' I changed the subject firmly.

'Let an old lady sit.' The Crone lowered her thickset body into an armchair then lifted her head. Her eyes were clouded with a milky film as she gazed at the stars for me. I fingered the potion bomb in my pocket, ready to defend her should an attack come. The roof was runed but you could never be too safe.

The long minutes drew out and I stifled the urge to fidget whilst I waited for the Goddess's verdict.

Abigay gave a little gasp and lowered her head as the white sheen vanished from her corneas. She cleared her throat and her dry voice rasped as she spoke. 'I do not know why, but the Goddess speaks of your Jake. Perhaps it is because we have just spoken of him. She tells me his thread was destined to be cut.' She frowned. 'That his thread was always meant to be cut sooner or later. As it was, you got later. I confess that I don't understand.'

I did, but I didn't want her to think about Jake; he was mine and I didn't want to share him in thought or deed. 'What about the griffin?' I asked impatiently.

'She is clear on that. You must help him or his young will die.'

'And would that be so bad?' I was playing devil's advocate. 'How many lives would I save by letting the murderess die?' I asked desperately. I didn't want to help Bastion. I wasn't against all griffins, just this one in particular – even if my conscience was telling me otherwise.

Abigay sighed again and looked at me like a stern teacher. 'The griffins bring balance. It is not their fault that they deal in death,' she chastened me. 'If you are ever to be accepted as the Symposium member, the coven council must know that you can put your personal feelings aside to do what is right. What is *needed*. The Goddess has gifted me sight of the many paths stretching before you, so trust me when I say you must save the griffin's child. It will put you on a path to true excellence. If you want to achieve your maximum potential, you must save her. On that path and that path alone will you create something that will revolutionise the Other realm. But first, you must save the griffin.'

I wanted to work with Bastion about as much as I wanted to poke myself in the eye with a hot needle, but I wanted excellence. I needed to succeed if only to prove my many detractors wrong. I was going to amount to *something*, damn it and damn them.

It looked like I'd be saving a griffin after all.

Chapter 3

I was deep in sleep when my warding runes blared, jerking me awake and sending my heart careening. I grabbed my athame and potion bomb from the bedside table and stumbled into my living room. I took a moment to consult with the warding runes and thrust my magic out to them. The warning had come from the balcony; although the intruder was out there, he or she had yet to come inside my flat.

I threw out my senses and found something distinctively griffin-ish: Bastion. If the impatient bastard thought that accosting me in the night was a way to secure my assistance, he had another think coming.

I inched carefully towards the balcony as I let my eyes adjust to the darkness, then frowned. There was nothing there. I reached out to the window and touched one of the warding runes. It lit up, still shining red. Something was still out there.

A griffin couldn't become invisible but a wizard could.

A wizard's magic is so much easier than a witch's – far less elegant, of course, but easier. All their magic requires is the IR, the Intention and Release; they *will* a thing and then they release that intention, either with a word or gesture, and it happens. Simple. Boring. Wizards don't need to know the runes, to know the interplay between them. There is no mastery or skill to their magic.

Different types of wizard can do different things. Some can heal; others can wipe your mind of your very thoughts and memories. At the start of my mum's illness that's what I thought had happened to her, but wizard after wizard had

tested her and denied the involvement of the IR.
It was just dementia, they said.

There was nothing *just* about it.

A movement caught my eye, a flutter in the
darkness. I pressed closer to the glass to see it.
Not a griffin, not a wizard wrapped in the IR. A
crow, its midnight-black feathers flashing in the
moonlight.

I checked the ward rune again: just one intruder.
I frowned; how had I felt it was a griffin when it
was just a bird? Of course, griffins are half-eagle,
so maybe the bird's energy had thrown me off?

I checked the surroundings one last time before
I unlocked my balcony door and slid it open. Cool
air rushed in and the crow fluttered weakly in
panic. 'It's okay,' I cooed. 'I'm here to help.'

I looked around the balcony then checked the
sky; in the Other realm, the sky is as dangerous
as the land. Dragons, griffins and even deadlier
creatures like the phoenix rule them. My mother
taught me that if it flew, it was deadly.

Mum had introduced me into the Other realm when I was six, which was young by many standards. I had grown up knowing I was a witch but she had started to teach me runes and potions from a tender age. While other children were learning to read, I was already devouring grimoires.

It is inconvenient to ferry back and forth between the Other and the Common realms, but it's a necessary evil. If you are on the human side – witches, wizards, werewolves, elementals, vampyrs and the like – then once you are introduced to the Other realm you have to go between the realms forever. That's where the creatures – dragons, dryads, ogres, satyrs, centaurs – have the advantage because they don't *need* to go to the Common realm. They can exist wholly in the Other if they want to. I had long since decided it was this disparity that was at the heart of all human-creature tensions.

We humans have to charge our magical batteries in the ordinary world – the Common realm – ready for use in the magical world – the Other realm. The Other realm co-exists with the Common realm and they run concurrently. The way I explain the realms to new witches is that it's as if you are short-sighted and suddenly you're handed glasses. When you're in the Common, you are minus your glasses and blind to the magical dangers around you. When you step through the portal into the Other realm, it is like putting on your glasses; suddenly you can *see* everything around you. You see a lilac sky instead of blue, turquoise grass instead of green, and a host of creatures – fire elementals, dragons, ogres – everything magical is revealed to you. And naturally, you have full access to your magic too. Suddenly the runes can actually light up and *do* something.

I looked at the crow and remembered Mum's warning: if it flies, it's dangerous. Then I scoffed at myself. It was a *crow*.

I knelt next to the panicked avian, which was bigger than I'd first thought, and flicked my eyes to its tail. The feathers flared out in a diamond shape, so it was not a crow but a raven. Its wings hung uselessly by its sides; they had been snapped. A chill ran through me. This was no accident; someone had snapped this bird's wings out of cruelty or for sport.

Black witches use pain to fuel some of their darker spells; was this evidence of a black witch in my coven? And how had the raven arrived on my balcony? It must have come from close by because it couldn't have flown far. By the Goddess, was a black witch amongst us?

I put the mystery aside for now and focused on helping the poor thing. 'I'm going to pick you up,' I warned it gently.

It gave a 'kraa', which I took as assent, and I slid both hands underneath its body. Supporting its broken wings, I gently lifted it and carried it into my open-plan living room and kitchen diner. It was heavier than I'd anticipated but I carried it easily. I laid it down on the wooden dining table, apologising all the while. Then I opened the refrigerator behind me and pulled out two of my strongest healing potions. I'd have to use them both sparingly with such a small creature.

I unfastened the lid of the potion jar and selected one of my smallest paintbrushes from the neatly laid out array. Dipping the brush into the dark-green pain-relieving potion, I painted on an activation rune, *isa,* over the site of each injury, one on each wing and one on the body just to be safe.

Each rune needs certain lines to fit the rune shape, but each witch paints them a little differently – a thicker line here, an embellishment there. We all have our own rune style. Mine is pretty much fuss-free because I want to do the job as quickly as possible, not worry about swirls and whorls to make it pretty. That really exasperated my mother; she favoured a certain "witchy" aesthetic.

I pulled my magic to me, reached out and activated the *isa* rune. As my magic ran through the delicate lines I'd painted on the raven, it gave the tiniest tug and the runes flared.

'Kraa,' the raven murmured, resting its head against the table.

'I'm glad that's a bit better. Now I need to heal your wings.' I paused. 'That might not feel so nice.' Some people might have felt idiotic speaking to a bird, but with so many familiars bopping about in the coven it wasn't wise to assume that the creature before me was a normal raven. Even if it was, all birds in the corvid family are smart. This one was probably not smart enough to understand human language, but perhaps my tone was enough; corvids aren't called the Einsteins of the bird family for nothing.

I grabbed a fresh paintbrush – it wouldn't do for the bonesetter to mix with the pain reliever. This time I dunked the brush in more generously because I had numerous runes to paint: *uruz*, the power rune, *halgaz*, the rune for illness, and then *sowilo,* the rune for healing. Finally I added *gebo,* the rune for a gift. I was gifting my magic to the raven. I didn't demand anything in return – mostly because the raven didn't have a bank account.

I channelled my magic through the delicate lines and the runes shone. The raven shrieked as its bones snapped back into place. 'Sorry,' I said as I stroked its head. 'But you're all done now. Get up and see how you feel.'

The raven really did seem to understand me. It hopped up, stretched out its wings to an impressive span of nearly a metre and a half, then flapped cautiously before lifting off and happily flying around my lounge. As it gained in confidence, it did a barrel roll.

I smiled at its antics. 'You're all good now. Can you hop back down here? I want to see if I can work out who hurt you.'

The raven landed as requested, and I wondered if it was indeed someone's familiar. I pushed down the old ache that thought gave me. Every witch on the planet has a familiar except me. But that is fine because I don't need an animal scrabbling around at my feet. If I say it enough times, maybe one day it will be true.

'One more rune, if I may. Stay still, please.' The raven sat patiently, claws holding the edge of my table as I re-sealed the potions I'd used and put them back in my fridge. Next I pulled out another potion and painted on *pethro*, the rune for revelation and secrets. My magic pulled a little as the rune activated and I saw a magic signature hanging before me, invisible to all eyes but the rune maker's.

My stomach lurched. It was definitely a witch's signature. It wasn't one that I recognised, but that didn't mean I didn't know the witch. It looked like the Crone might find a black witch on her hunt after all.

Chapter 4

I had stumbled back to bed after opening the balcony door to let out the raven but my eyes still felt gritty. I'd struggled to sleep after the raven incident. The only way I could imagine that the raven had reached my balcony was by escaping from a witch nearby. I had a bunch of witches close by, a whole tower block of them to be precise. We might have a black witch in our midst and that thought – that *failure* – had me tossing and turning until exhaustion finally claimed me.

My alarm beeped, pulling me out of a disturbing dream full of black robes and discordant chanting. I showered perfunctorily, scrubbing sleep from my skin and my brain. It had been a whole two weeks since I'd been to the Common realm and my skin was itching, a sure sign I needed to recharge. I'd been putting it off but now I needed to go, especially if I was going to scry for the damned griffin.

As I did every morning, I braided my damp hair to get it out of the way then took my strongest protection potion and painted on some runes. The 'protection from fire' runes would reduce a third-degree burn to a first-degree one, though they couldn't protect me completely. If a fire elemental held a flame on me for long enough, eventually the runes would shatter and I'd burn like anyone else. No matter how good my runes are, I'm not immune to fire like the dragons.

But the runes were better than nothing, especially if I was going to the Common realm where I would be stripped of my magic. I took the time to paint anti-vampyr runes on my neck, wrists and inner thighs – vampyrs so love a pulse point. Then I pulled out my magic and let it run along the rune lines. A firm tug made the runes shine once and then disappear so they were invisible to the naked eye.

It was early, but I'd get to Rosie's just as it opened so I could slip in and out of the portal before the rest of the Other realm was even stirring. Gritty eyes aside, there are advantages to being an early bird. I texted my substitute father, Oscar, and asked him to meet me in the garage in ten minutes. He's Mum's partner, and he replied straight away as he always does. Oscar has my back.

I had a glass of water and a banana to start my day right. Later I'd have a cappuccino and a blueberry muffin to start my day wrong.

Oscar was in the car with the engine running by the time I walked into the garage. His blue eyes warmed when he saw me and his lips tipped up into a smile that I returned. Despite his salt-and-pepper hair and the lines on his face, he still doesn't look like a man in his sixties. I dread to think what I'll do when he retires as my driver and bodyguard.

I slipped into the back of the car and fastened my seatbelt. 'Morning, Oscar. Did you sleep well?' I asked as a yawn cracked my face.

'Not too badly, Am. You?'

I scrubbed my eyes. 'I had a visit from a raven.'

His white eyebrows shot up. 'A raven?'

'Some black witch had snapped its wings for fun or for a ritual. I don't know.'

He grimaced. 'Abigay might find a black witch after all,' he said, reiterating my own worries.

'And won't that look great for me?' I grimaced.

'The council can't blame you for one bad apple,' he pointed out optimistically. 'Maybe it was an accident. A strong gust of wind and a bad landing.' He didn't believe that any more than I did.

'We'll see. To Rosie's please, and then afterwards we can visit Mum. When did you last recharge?'

Oscar put the car in gear and we rolled out of the garage. 'Last night. I'll be good for a while,' he promised.

We lapsed into comfortable silence as we drove to the hall housing the portal. Oscar toggled on some soothing classical music. He was young when he and my mum got together and some had called her a cradle-snatcher – though not loudly because my mum has a fiery temper and is a dab hand at offensive runes. I was a teenager at the time, but I suspect that their relationship spanned several years before that.

When they were outed, Oscar quit the Connection and came to work full time for the coven. After all these years, he still refused to tell me what he'd done for the Connection. 'If I told you, I'd have to kill you,' the wizard joked. So, some sort of black ops, I was guessing.

We parked outside of Rosie's café, the front for the portal hall, and waited patiently for the lights to come on to show that it was officially open for business. I love to watch the sun warming the lilac skies, so I braced myself for the blue skies of the Common realm that I'd soon be seeing. I always miss the lilac when I'm in the Common, and the grass looks weird to me. It has a strange shade of green rather than the turquoise colour it is in the Other realm. Many things in the realms are the same, but the different colour palette is a constant reminder of which realm you are in.

When the lights blazed on, I went in. Oscar lingered at the entrance where he could keep an eye on everyone who came and went while I went straight to the portal. I nodded to Maxwell, the guardian of the hall. The fire elemental was cleaning down the café's surfaces like he would if he was a real café owner.

Rosie's is a hub of Other activity and it sells drinks and food like a real café. It also doubles as a hotel for those rich enough – and paranoid enough – to merit an overnight stay and a full team of fire elementals guarding them whilst they are vulnerable in the Common realm.

'Morning, Miss DeLea,' Maxwell called respectfully, flames dancing on his head.

I nodded acknowledgement and kept on going to the back room. It was discreetly marked with the symbol for the Other realm: three triangles inside each other, surrounded by a circle. I opened the door, strolled inside and immediately walked back out.

Maxwell was still cleaning the counter but now the flames on his head had been replaced by a mop of stylish blond hair. My Other realm glasses had been removed, leaving me unable to see the magic that still existed around me. Maxwell was still in the Other realm with fire dancing on his head, but I couldn't see it no matter how hard I tried. He could shish-kebab me where I stood if he wanted to, though I knew he wouldn't because that would be incredibly bad for business. It wasn't a nice feeling and I found myself fingering the potion vial still in my pocket. I am a powerful witch and even in the Common realm I have access to the tiniest trickle of magic, enough to set off a potion bomb. I wasn't completely vulnerable, I told myself firmly. And, of course, I had Oscar.

I handed Maxwell my reusable plastic travel mug. 'My usual,' I ordered. It was always best to be brusque here because the portal halls double as the fire elementals' information-gathering sites, and any gossip and conversation would be reported back to Roscoe, the head of the Pit, the fire elementals' ruling body. You don't say anything in the halls that you don't want others to know, so I try to say as little as possible. My business is my own.

Maxwell slid across a cappuccino in my takeout cup and two blueberry muffins in a brown paper bag. I grabbed the food and drink, paid and left. Oscar slipped into place a step behind me, scanning the area for danger. Today there was none; the world was still sleeping.

We drove to Mum's care home and waited until 7am rolled around. I signed us both in at reception and we walked up to her room. Technically, visiting hours didn't start until 9.30am, but judicious bribes dressed up as voluntary overpayments meant I could come and go pretty much as I pleased. Mum had always been an early riser – hence my own habits – but any time before 7am made the care home staff grumpy, so I tried to arrive after that in order to stay under the radar.

I navigated the familiar corridors with ease and knocked firmly on Mum's door. 'Come in,' she called. Her voice sounded strong today and I tried to quash the hope rising inside me.

I walked in. She was already dressed and eating a bowl of cereal. Her ferret, Lucille, was draped around her shoulders. Lucille lifted her head and gave me a chitter then went back to snoozing against Mum. They both looked far older than they should have done; linked as they were, the illness was taking its toll on them both. Mum was seventy-one, but she looked like she was well into her eighties.

I didn't call her 'Mum'; instead I waited to see if she would greet me so that I would know if today was a good or bad day.

'Amber, darling. Sit down,' she snapped. 'Don't hover. You know I hate it when you hover.'

Relief swamped me. A good day, thank the Goddess. 'Hi, Mum, how are you?'

'Oh, you know.' She waved a hand. 'The staff keep taking away my paintbrushes. I've even started to *actually* paint just so they'll let me hold one. I did a lovely landscape picture yesterday.' She frowned. 'I've runed myself my whole life, so it's not right that I can't rune myself now. Strangers runing for me? I ask you!'

'Not strangers,' I reassured her. 'I rune for you every month. You're due a refresh next week.'

'Oh.' Luna simmered down. 'Well, of course I trust you, darling, but I still wish they'd let me do it myself. They made such a kerfuffle when I tried to brew a simple protection potion.'

The fuss had been justified. Luna had gone into the kitchen and knocked out the chef with a frying pan so that she could brew potions alone. She'd made a potion explode all over the kitchen before the other staff realised what she was doing, and she'd suffered third-degree burns. Her kitchen privileges had been revoked after that.

I made a non-committal noise. It was best not to argue with her.

'Who is this?' She gestured sharply at Oscar. 'He looks familiar.'

I saw the flash of grief in Oscar's eyes before it was gone. 'I'm Amber's bodyguard,' he lied calmly.

'It's Miss DeLea to you, then!' Luna snapped. 'Go and guard her body outside my room,' she ordered imperiously.

'Yes ma'am,' he responded, searching her eyes for some hint of recognition. When I was young, he would 'ma'am' her when he wanted to get a rise. 'I'll give you ma'am,' she would jokily reply.

'Well, don't just stand there! Out you go!' she said sharply.

Oscar dipped his head and left. I felt my heart twist in sympathy; it was his turn to be forgotten. These days, she tended to remember one of us but rarely both; some days it was neither of us.

I put the blueberry muffins on two plates for us – Mum can't abide eating out of paper bags. I sipped my cappuccino, ignoring her frown because it wasn't in a 'proper' mug.

We talked inconsequentially for a while. She seemed to be under the impression that I was in my twenties and still studying under a rune master, but I didn't correct her. I told her about the raven and Abigay's visit. I like to be open and honest about as much of my day as I can with her, without contradicting what she thinks she knows about me. Contradictions cause her distress, and I hate to see her like that. It hurts to see her lost.

'Oh! Abi must visit me.' Mum beamed. 'Tell her to come by when she gets a chance.'

I felt my own smile dim. Abigay *had* been by, but I didn't argue because it would distress Mum. I nodded. 'I will do,' I promised emptily.

'Good, good.' Her eyes fixed on me, suddenly sharp, urgent and lucid. She leaned forward, 'Has the prophecy come to pass yet?'

I blinked. 'What prophecy?'

She leaned back into her seat, nibbled on her blueberry muffin then smiled gently. 'What prophecy is that, dear?'

It was nearly enough to make me swear, though I'd only made the mistake of doing that once in front of Mum and never again. Whatever she'd been about to tell me, the moment was gone, lost to her illness. Grief crushed me; it was so unfair that she was alive and with me, but at the same time she was lost to me. I longed for my strong mother's return with all of my heart.

As if she had read my thoughts, she pierced me with a sharp stare. 'What are you going to accomplish today?' she asked as she had done virtually every day of my adolescent life. 'What are you going to do to make yourself proud?'

I thought for a moment before I squared my shoulders. 'I'm going to save someone's life.'

She beamed at me with pride. 'Good girl. Get to it then, Amber DeLea. Make the DeLea name sing.'

I was dismissed.

Chapter 5

It was still too early to return to Rosie's and the Other realm. Ideally I needed at least five hours in the Common realm for a strong enough recharge to keep me going for another week or so. Eight hours would give me two weeks' respite, but I was rarely patient enough for that.

Being in the Common realm makes the skin itch between my shoulder blades. I make it my business not to attract enemies, but danger is ever present. I prefer an overnight charge when I can, though I never pay Rosie's extortionate protection charges. I am safe enough in a coven of witches behind a wall of runes.

'Let's go to The Spice Shoppe,' I said to Oscar as I climbed into the back of the car.

He nodded and started the engine. We didn't engage in conversation; we never do after visiting Mum. We both need time to decompress.

It took us twenty minutes to get to High Wycombe. The Spice Shoppe professes to be an herb and spice specialist, selling more than 2,500 products. For most people, that's all it is – a source of great cooking ingredients – but for the local witches it is our apothecary. Here we can buy potion ingredients or pre-made potions. I have little need for the latter because I prefer to brew and stock my own. It isn't just a matter of trust, but of excellence; my potions are better. Even so, we often purchase potions for the coven's store from here, especially when my brewing time is limited.

Mum had been letting me brew since I was eight years old, by which point I was chomping at the bit to start potion making. I'd already gone through two years of home schooling, two years of learning about ingredients and their interactions, and I was desperate to create my own rather than follow the instructions of others. Mum had been proud of my creative streak and fostered it enthusiastically. She had worked two jobs to pay for all of the ingredients I needed.

It was only when I was older that I wondered exactly how she'd found the time to work both jobs. She was always there with me, teaching me, raising me, being both my mother and father and everything else I needed. I supposed she worked in the evenings; she had always insisted I go to bed early. I was allowed to read, as long as I didn't get up. It had seemed a fair deal at the time.

She must have been exhausted. I couldn't ask her about it now; I should have asked her more about it then, but I'd been too self-involved, too driven to prove myself to think about others.

The car rolled to a stop outside The Spice Shoppe. As we got out, I checked my surroundings. I frowned at the large black bird that had settled on the powerlines above my head. Was it the raven from the night before? It saw me looking up and gave a 'kraa' in welcome. Hmm. Had it followed me here?

I dismissed the raven from my thoughts as Oscar and I went into the shop. The smell was enough to make the tension drain from my shoulders. Herbs and spices mingled in the air, tantalising my nose and awakening my senses. I grabbed a basket and started wandering around. I had no need of a shopping list; I always knew the state of my private stores.

I selected some mothercap and some vervain then spied a fresh delivery of Jamaican dogwood, some cramp bark, black cohosh, eleuthero and skullcap. I found sarsaparilla, rhodiola and smilax. This was exactly what I needed to while away an hour or two. I hummed happily in my head but made sure no noises escaped my throat – that would have been embarrassing.

I didn't bother with the hidden potions store at the back. I knew from the shop's daily emails that there wasn't anything new and revolutionary in stock. New potions are few and far between these days as modern conveniences reduce the need to turn to magical solutions.

After losing myself in the rows of herbs and spices, I reluctantly went to the checkout. No one shops here for free – not me, not the coven council, not even the Crone. All witches pay their way and the proceeds from sales go towards supporting any covens that are particularly in need. I was proud of the fact that I had never once had to make an application for formal assistance. My coven was self-supporting, though it was notable that some of the witches were bringing in far more income than others. Briony Fields was being especially lackadaisical, though Melrose Samper wasn't far behind. They were both on my naughty list for monitoring, together with Timothy Woodman.

John Melton personally rang up my purchases and gave me a deferential bow, which I appreciated. 'You have an excellent eye. You've picked out the finest specimens.'

'As always, there are only the finest specimens to be found here.' I returned the compliment, finishing our well-worn dance.

'You're too kind, Coven Mother, too kind.' He bobbed his bow again and touched his hand to his heart.

I didn't even wince at the four-figure number he rang through; I just passed him my card. Most of my savings are earmarked for potion ingredients because potions are my passion, my hobby. Creating new ones is what I do for fun. I'm the life and soul of the party if you get me talking about ingredient interactions.

I stacked my two cardboard boxes, picked them up and headed out with my arms full. My back gave a slight twinge and I reminded myself to do more yoga. My body needs me to make the effort these days now that youth is no longer on my side.

I could see Oscar itching to help me carry the boxes, but we'd agreed long ago that it was far better for him to have his hands free to keep me safe than to help me with my shopping, even if it went against his every gentlemanly urge.

I scanned the blue skies but I couldn't see the raven. Maybe it had been a coincidence – but I don't like coincidences. Oscar unlocked the car and I popped the precious cargo into the footwell of the front seat where nothing would roll around and get damaged.

'Rosie's?' Oscar enquired. He knows me well; I needed my magic back. I checked the time. It was gone lunchtime, nearly 1pm, and I'd managed a whole six hours in Common. Not bad – including the drive back, I'd be close to seven hours recharging. It would have to do. 'Please,' I confirmed.

Once I was ensconced in the car, I checked my diary on my phone. I tried to keep my schedule clear while the triune were visiting, which allowed me to catch up on paperwork, but I was itching to do something useful. No one had emailed anything urgent, so it looked like helping the griffins would have to do.

I grimaced, then sent a text message to Bastion. *Come to the tower at 2.30pm and I will scry for your missing griffin. Bring something dear to her with you.*

I received a response almost immediately: *I'll be there.*

I sniffed at his lack of effusive thanks. The griffin had no manners. I'd have to teach him some.

Chapter 6

At 2pm I went to my coven office at the base of the tower block. I had preparations to carry out which I did not want or need my 'client' to see. My magic was back, swirling around me happily like a warm breeze on a summer's day. I love that sensation. Feeling secure again, I dismissed Oscar for the day; I was as safe as I could be in the tower, even with a deadly griffin assassin as my next appointment. Plus Oscar is at my beck and call day and night and he deserved some down time. I try to release him whenever I can.

Failing to prepare was preparing to fail, as my mother always said, so I gathered everything I would need to conduct the scry. I cleaned my porcelain bowl to make sure no impurities remained and ran the water I would use twice through a filter. I still possessed a plentiful supply of potions but I checked them over, just to be sure. Each scrying is different, so I thought carefully about which potions I'd want to apply to the griffin's object. Finally I selected three: a sight potion, a guidance one and a communication one. They would work cohesively with the runes I had in mind, though I'd do a rune reading beforehand to be sure.

I set out the potions and selected a number of paintbrushes of different sizes. Which one I used would depend on the size of the object in question. I put some latex gloves on my work desk, ready to use later; they were wholly unnecessary but added to the impression that potions weren't to be toyed with. Anyone can paint a rune using a potion and achieve a modicum of magic, though obviously that's not something we witches shout about, but it takes a true witch to activate the runes' greatest power.

I carefully spread out a rune cloth on my desk. Next, I took the bag containing my rose-quartz rune stones, pulled them out and held the naked stones to my heart for a minute. I closed my eyes and thought of Bastion and his need to see his daughter. I kept my eyes closed as I cast the stones onto their cloth.

I opened my eyes and examined the rune cloth, then selected the five runes on which the stones had landed in the centre. I nodded, satisfied. That would be a strong combination. I turned back to my desk – and was unable to stifle the gasp that was pulled from my lips.

Legs splayed in an irritating display of male dominance, Bastion was lounging in my guest chair. I hadn't heard so much as a whisper of movement. I reached out to my warding runes – they were still green. The griffin had, no doubt been to the reception desk and acquired a guest rune which, when painted on him, ensured that he didn't trip every ward he went near. I was glad he was observing the formalities, but a damned knock on the door would have been nice.

'Didn't your mother teach you to knock?' I snarled.

He smiled. 'No.' He said nothing more, just gave me that intense look.

'Do you have the object?' I demanded abruptly. I wasn't going to engage in small talk with him of all people.

He gestured to my desk, which now held a large, ceremonial-looking dagger. Naturally, a griffin's favourite object would be a weapon.

I busied myself with the rest of my preparations. I poured the purified water into my porcelain bowl and took the dagger to my work table and unsheathed it. I handled the blade with care; no doubt it was sharp and deadly.

Selecting the smallest paintbrush, I pulled on my purple latex gloves and opened the lids from the three potions I'd chosen. I began to paint the runes from the earlier rune spread onto the blade's surface. First *ansuz*, the estuary rune, for communication, then *nauthiz* for need and *isa* for clarity. Finally I painted on *perthro* for the unknown and *kenaz*, the torch rune, for guidance.

It is for this reason that scrying is so expensive. Each scry is wholly unique to the client and the person being scried – you can't simply repeat the same runes and see what happens. The covens charge nearly enough for a down payment on a house to undertake a scrying because it is something no other magical creature can do, not a seer or a wizard or an empath. The size of the bill I'd be sending the griffin made me happy, even though I knew he was more than good for it, damn him.

I murmured the activation words and pulled my magic forward along the rune lines. When they shone, I carefully lowered the dagger into the brimming porcelain bowl. Water splashed onto the floor as it was displaced but I ignored it, focusing instead on the caress of my magic. The runes painted onto the blade lifted up from it and swirled on the water's surface.

I waited to see the image of another griffin form on the water, but the runes continued to swirl and whirl around, moving ceaselessly. The scry had failed. Nothing is ever easy. The griffin we were seeking had been warded against scrying. I was now almost certain that Charlize had been taken somewhere against her will.

Bastion stood, walked to the edge of my office and pulled back his fist. His muscles rippled and bunched – and then he punched the wall. His fist smashed right through the bricks, making a hole in my office right next to the window.

My mouth dropped open. He'd been under the witch's curse for weeks now so he should have been weaker than that. 'I'll add the repair costs to the bill,' I said evenly, like I wasn't fazed by him disembowelling my wall.

'You do that,' he said, just as evenly. He sounded calm and collected, though I suspected he was neither.

I'm not a complete monster; although I don't have children, I could empathise with Bastion's anxiety for his daughter. Given our circumstances, Jake and I couldn't have children. It hadn't felt right to raise children in a world where they would have to be hidden away with their father. But truthfully, I have never had any interest in having a child. I've never experienced any maternal urges and I've long since lost patience in justifying my life choices to others. I ignore the looks of pity, the comments about me never experiencing the all-consuming love of a parent for a child. Fine. I don't need all-consuming love. Look where it gets you: abandoned by a husband and alone with a child. No, thank you. I'm happy to focus on making my mark on the world, making my time on this earth *matter.* I will leave the child rearing to those who have room in their hearts, for I have none.

Looking at the tension in Bastion's shoulders, the stress he was under, I was grateful for my lack of offspring. Perhaps that made me selfish, but there was no one in my life to worry about. I could be as selfish as I liked and there was no one to care.

'There must be something else you can do.' Bastion's voice was low and gravelly.

I stopped the denial before it passed my lips. The Crone had been clear: it wasn't enough to merely *try* to find the griffin; if I wanted to walk on the path to excellence, I *needed* to find her.

There was more I could do but I needed to think about it. There was a price for what I was contemplating – and I wasn't sure I wanted to pay it.

Chapter 7

Bastion was still looking at me with pleading in his eyes. If anything, that made me even less inclined to help him. He hadn't stopped to help *me* when he had taken Jake from this world. 'I will consider the further steps available to us and I will be in touch in due course,' I said finally.

He looked surprised; he had obviously expected a flat denial. Ha! I love to subvert expectations. 'Thank you.'

'I'm not doing it for you,' I replied harshly, and I really wasn't. Nor was I doing it for his daughter. I was doing it for myself so I could take the path that I wanted to be on. Okay – maybe there was also a smidge of compassion for his poor daughter. I could remember all too well what it felt like to be taken against your will, because I'd been kidnapped by some werewolves and they'd threatened to kill me. Lucy and her wolves, with Bastion's help, had saved me. But that wasn't personal; Bastion didn't care about me and I didn't owe him anything.

I wondered who I was trying to convince. Shut up, Jiminy.

Bastion nodded. 'Nevertheless, you have my thanks, witch. Let me know what you need for the next steps and I will secure it.' His tone was arrogant and certain, and I was tempted to ask him for the crown jewels just to make him dance to my tune. Instead, I held open my door. He left, his daughter's dagger secured at his hip.

I cleaned up after the failed scry and poured away the water and potions. I washed the latex gloves, and removed them, ready to be used again; there was no need to add to the planet's plastic waste. Then I phoned Jeb in maintenance and told him to fix the hole in my wall. Pronto. He gushed promises and I hung up on him midstream. Time is money.

I went upstairs to my penthouse suite and started to close the curtains. As I approached my balcony, I saw the raven calmly sitting there, cool as a cucumber. It made my heart flutter with an old hope. Maybe the raven *could* be my familiar.

I slid open the balcony door. 'Hello again,' I greeted him with a smile.

'Kraa.'

'What are you doing back here?' He tilted his head to look at me. 'Would you mind awfully if I did a quick test on you? It won't hurt,' I promised.

'Kraa,' he agreed.

I reached out with my magic to the raven but nothing happened. Something was in the way – another bond. He was already someone else's familiar. Disappointment welled up suddenly and strongly, making my throat feel scratchy and full. How could I have thought I'd finally get a familiar after all this time? It was something that had always been denied me. Love of any kind was forbidden to me; even Jake had been distant in the end. We'd been best friends before he died but nothing more. There'd been nothing like *that* since the attack, though in my mind we'd been all but wed. For better or worse. We'd had worse in spades.

I rubbed my eyes, which were suddenly hot and full of tears that I wanted to ignore. I wasn't sure if they were for Jake or for myself. I was achingly alone, and even the comfort of a familiar was denied me.

I wished Jinx wasn't on her honeymoon. I toyed with the idea of ringing Lucy, but our friendship was new and delicate. To be honest, I had no idea how to manage a friendship. Besides, Lucy was busy trying to cement her position as an alpha werewolf with a queenly title. She didn't need me moaning that I was lonely. I was forty-two for the

Godess's sake. I'd been lonely for most of my life; you'd think I'd be used to it by now.

All this self-pity was enough to straighten my backbone. I didn't need anyone, and I didn't need a familiar. I was going to achieve greatness alone. I was going to make the world *better*. I wiped the tears from my cheeks. 'Sorry,' I muttered to the bird. 'I was hoping you might be my familiar but you're already somebody else's.'

'Kraa,' the raven agreed. He spread his wings and flew from the balcony into my open plan living space.

I followed him in. 'Shouldn't you go home?'

The raven flew once around the room before settling on my shoulder. He was surprisingly heavy – a couple of kilograms at least – but his presence was oddly soothing. He reached out with his black beak, picked at some stray auburn hairs that had come loose from my plait and tucked them neatly around my ear like he was weaving a nest.

'Oh, thank you.' I looked at the bird resting on my left shoulder. 'Well, if you're sticking about for a while, I can't call you "raven" the whole time. What about … Fehu? It's the rune for luck.' The newly-named Fehu gave a happy hop on my shoulder, making me smile. I fancied that he approved of the name. 'Fehu, it is.'

I dug around in my kitchen and found some ham for him. Part of all witches' education is learning how to look after their familiars and I'd spent many hours poring over animal books, daydreaming about an animal that would love me exclusively. I knew about their care – and avians had always been a favourite of mine. As a kid, I'd even daydreamed about bonding with the phoenix – that would have shown my bullies if I'd bonded with a deadly bird. Ha! That would have stopped them muttering that I didn't have a soul for anything to bond with.

'Are you staying or going?' I asked Fehu and nodded at the open balcony door. He just looked at me. Staying, then.

Someone's familiar or not, something in me trusted this bird. It was rare for me to experience trust, so I wondered if the Goddess was guiding me. Was it wise to trust Fehu? My gut said yes. Finally, I shut the balcony door and closed the curtains. I wasn't in the mood for wrestling with a bird and I really didn't want to hurt his newly healed wings by trying to bundle him out without his consent. Respecting autonomy and consent is important, even with animals.

I bolted my front door; it's not paranoia if they *are* out to get you. Once my home was secure I checked my runes were in order, paying special attention to the privacy ones. From an early age my mum had drilled it into me that no one must find out about our family grimoire, not even Aunt Abigay. With the privacy runes activated nothing inside these walls could be revealed.

I went into my bedroom and opened one of the cupboards to reveal a metal safe behind a wooden door. I unlocked it, giving my childhood stuffed toy – a cat called Megan – a quick hug to my heart, then I set Megan back safely on the shelves and carefully retrieved the book from the safe.

The DeLea family grimoire is ancient. The pages are yellow with age and the leather bindings are scratched and worn, with runes carved into its very skin. I stroked the book's spine but it remained unresponsive and I grimaced. It had been sleeping for too long. It would need blood to wake it up.

I opened the drawer in my bedside cabinet. Where others might have sex toys or underwear, I keep my crystal ball, my athame, my lancet and my private rune stones. I picked up the lancet and quickly pierced my forefinger so that a small drop of blood welled up, then stroked my finger down the book's spine again. The small drop of blood pulsed once and was gone. The book rose into the air of its own volition.

'Hi, Grimmy,' I said to the ancient grimoire, the childhood nickname slipping from my lips.

'Why, Miss Amber! What a pleasure it is to hear your voice after all this time.' Grimmy spoke with an American gentleman's drawl; he'd spent a century or two in the Deep South with my ancestors. He loved to talk of his time in Alabama, though the less said about his time in Salem the better. He'd been in the UK for more than three hundred years, but he clings to his drawl like Rose to that wooden plank in the *Titanic*. Even after all this time, I have no idea how he projects his voice into the world.

Fehu shifted uneasily on my shoulder and gave a hard 'caw' as he glared at the book. Somehow he could hear the voice too; I suspected Grimmy was projecting his words straight into our minds, though the thought of something inanimate inside my brain was disconcerting.

'Miss Amber – you have a familiar! After all this time! What a delight! What a pleasure! Why I always told your dear mother, Miss Luna, that—'

'Fehu isn't my familiar,' I interjected. 'He's someone else's. He's just ... hanging out.'

'Ah. Well.' Disappointment rang in Grimmy's voice but he battled it and tried to keep his tone upbeat. 'That's fine. You don't need a familiar, Miss Amber,' he backtracked. 'A familiar is just one more creature to scuttle underfoot.'

'Mm-hmm.'

Grimmy cleared his non-existent throat and tried to change the subject. 'How is Miss Luna?'

'She's a little worse than she was when we last spoke,' I admitted.

'I'm sorry to hear that. I'd love to visit with her one day.'

No way in hell. 'I've told you it would be too much for her.'

'No doubt, no doubt. So why have you woken me? Not just for a little *tête-a-tête*, I surmise.'

'No.' I took a deep breath. 'I tried to scry for someone but it failed. I need some alternative way to locate them.'

There was a long moment of silence. 'You've had scries fail before and not come stroking my spine.'

'I know. But the stars – the Goddess – said I need to find this particular person to achieve greatness.'

'Ah. If there's something my little Miss Amber wants, it's greatness.' Grimmy paused. 'There's a price, Miss Amber. You know it.'

I nodded, then realised the book probably couldn't see me. 'I know it. How much?' I always let Grimmy draw the line in the sand for his opening gambit; it is always outrageous.

'For something like this? Six months, my dear, at the least.'

That wasn't as bad as I'd feared, but I protested because it was what he expected. 'Six months!'

I blustered. 'That's ridiculous. One week.' My counter offer.

'One week? Why, now you're just being insulting, my dear. I've half a mind to go right back to sleep,' he huffed, mock affronted. He would do no such thing; he needed the deal as much as I did. I waited. 'Three months, and that's my final offer,' he spat. If he'd had arms, they would have been crossed huffily.

'One month. And that's as good as it gets.'

'Six weeks and done,' he offered.

I suppressed a surge of triumph. Not a bad result. 'And done. Payment on completion of the task.'

'Why, you insult me, you young whippersnapper! Of course the task will be done, darn it.'

'Then it's no problem to include the condition. You get six weeks of my life force and in exchange you guarantee that we will locate this griffin.'

The book sighed. 'You didn't say anything about it being a damned creature.'

'Grimmy...' My tone was heavy with disapproval.

'I know, I know. You've told me often enough about your modern utopian society where creatures and humans rub shoulders. Scandalous, if you ask me.'

'I'm not asking you. Do you want your six weeks or not?'

'You were nicer as a child,' Grimmy muttered. 'Fine. As it happens, I have a number of locator spells in my pages. How dark do you want to go?'

'As light and fluffy as you can,' I replied firmly. Becoming a black witch is a slippery slope, one Mum had warned me against time and time again. It isn't the use of blood that is the issue but the use of pain, even though pain is more efficacious. Obviously, most bloodlettings come with pain, but using the pain with the blood can be a problem. That, and the fact that blood working can be addictive. The more blood you use in a working, the more you slip.

I am a white witch, which is something I cling to despite my ancestry being peppered with black witches. Grimmy's existence is evidence enough of that. There are things I won't do, that I won't compromise on, and this was one of them.

I would never use another's pain to fuel a spell. I'd find the griffin and achieve greatness – but not by sacrificing my soul.

Chapter 8

In the end we compromised: the spell was darker than I wanted and lighter than Grimmy wanted. Neither of us was happy but it was the sweet spot of compromise. Misery loves company.

It is rare for me to imbibe a potion rather than rune with one, but there are some exceptions. The hydration potion is multifaceted; it will help you if you are dangerously dehydrated or if you've lost too much blood. I was about to use it for the latter purpose. Grimmy's spell required blood in order to work, a whole litre of it. Since I refused to harm an animal to get that blood, it would have to come from me.

The hydration potion isn't one I keep on hand, so I headed downstairs to the coven common room. It was after school and before dinnertime, so the coven kids had claimed the couch and were sitting in a puddle of happy limbs. I looked them over, noting that nobody was being left out. I wished an adult had taken such care of me when I was young. Mum had been more focused on my studies than on me making friends.

Meredith, one of my more studious witches, was sitting at the dining room table studying rune interactions. She had a notepad beside her. I nodded and she beamed back. 'Hard at work I see,' I commented approvingly.

'Yes, Coven Mother,' she smiled. It always feels weird to be called 'mother' by someone who is virtually my own age. Meredith looked over anxiously to check on her daughter, Ria, the one I'd caught canoodling with Henry.

'She's fine,' I reassured her. 'She's slouched down with Henry.'

Meredith relaxed. 'Thank you, Mother.'

I nodded and went past her to the coven's potion store. It was manned by a very bored-looking Briony Fields who was slumped on a chair, one leg up, one down, scrolling aimlessly on her phone. I frowned. She wasn't supposed to be doom scrolling on her phone, she was supposed to be checking the dates on the potions and noting what stock was running low. Not all witches choose to brew their own potions like me. 'Briony,' I said.

She jumped up and dropped her phone. 'Oh! Coven Mother! You don't often come down here.' She laughed nervously.

'I do not. Phones are banned whilst you are manning the potion store, Briony, you know that. If you're bored and can't bring yourself to do a stock take, then bring a book. *Learn* something,' I chastised.

'Yes, Coven Mother.' She looked at her feet.

I pressed my lips together and swept past her into the store. Someone other than Briony had been tidying up. The store looked neat, though as I glanced around I saw a couple of potions nearing their expiry date. They should have been placed in the fridge to maximise their remaining use or disposed of. I frowned. I should come down here more often and do spot checks, but Ethan runs the store and his ego rivals mine. Even so, we would be bumping heads soon if he thought this standard was acceptable.

I went to the back of the store to retrieve a hydration potion. There were only four vials left and my frown deepened. Things were going to heck in a hand-basket. Ten vials of a life-saving potion was the minimum number allowed at any one given time. This was *not* good enough.

I pocketed two vials, bringing the stock down to a measly two, and stalked to the potion logbook. A quick scan told me that the hydration potion had been fully restocked only last month. Fifty vials had been logged in, so no way should stocks be so low. My gut clenched. Someone was using the potion for the same purpose as me: blood recovery. And that meant that, in all likelihood, we did indeed have a black witch in our midst. Damn it.

I made a note to say I had removed the hydration potions then scanned the log. Despite a large number of vials being missing, no other withdrawals of the hydration potion were noted. Crikey. I didn't run half as tight a ship as I thought. This was unacceptable.

I fired off blistering emails to Ethan and Jeb, demanding that they undertake a full review of the potion stores – and the logs – immediately and personally. I cc'd Oscar; he might not be a witch but he'd make sure a thorough check was carried out.

I glared at Briony as I walked out. 'Ethan and Jeb will both be here soon. The store is in an appalling state. I expect you to assist them in bringing it up to standard.'

She gulped. 'Yes, Coven Mother.'

I swept out and headed back to my apartment. The whole building was drenched in shadows, which matched my dark mood. I stalked into my room and started ranting to Grimmy and Fehu. They both let me get my frustration off my chest and stayed silent whilst I bitched about other people's poor attention to detail. This was what happened when I allowed myself to delegate! The checks and balances were put in place for a *reason,* so that we could keep track of too much potion use.

Some witches brew their own like me, but if they use the potion store's ingredients then that also merits investigation. Few of them have my financial resources and most can't drop several thousand pounds on ingredients without blinking. It wasn't beyond the realm of possibility that someone was undertaking coven work off the books to fund their illicit habit. Goddess damn it, all it took was one rotten apple and before you knew it you had a black coven undertaking animal – or worse, human – sacrifices. Not. On. My. Watch.

I fumed, battling to get my temper into check. Grimmy spoke into one of my lengthier pauses. 'A glass of wine, Miss Amber? To calm the nerves, perhaps?'

'My nerves are fine,' I snapped. 'I'm going to kick someone's bum for this. If they drag my reputation down—' or ruined my chance of becoming the next Symposium member '—then the Goddess help them. Rune ruin! This is a mess.'

'If I may suggest,' Grimmy drawled, 'perhaps we should focus on one problem at a time? Let's find this missing griffin, shall we?' The book had a point.

I went to my bedside table to get the athame. The blade was sharp and I could feel Grimmy's anticipation. 'A litre of blood now, darling,' he whispered.

I nodded grimly. Bloodletting is not my favourite pastime, but it was necessary for this spell. I set out everything I needed and rolled back the rug on my living-room floor to reveal the carefully painted pentagram on the floorboards. I set one candle at each point of the rune and lit them, then studiously followed Grimmy's instructions and painted rune after rune into the triangle points of the pentagram.

It took an hour. Fehu flew around in agitation after each triangle was completed. I guessed all this stuff was bringing back bad memories. 'I'm not going to hurt you,' I reassured him. 'I'm going to hurt me.'

'Kraa,' he agreed. He hopped onto my sofa and wandered back and forth along it. He gave a warning burble.

'It's okay. We're nearly done.' I wasn't sure who I was reassuring, him or me.

When the pentagram had been runed to Grimmy's specifications, I went to the bathroom with my athame and wooden bowl. I have a number of potions in there. Some are purely for vanity's sake; keeping my skin looking youthful and glowing is one of my few vices. As well as my beauty-maximising potions, which I designed myself, I also have healing potions.

If I had to do bloodletting, I wanted to do it without an audience in a place that was easy to clean. I rolled up my bathmat and sat on the floor. I held my left forearm steady whilst I made a sharp incision with my athame. The blade cut into my flesh, making me gasp and sway. Ugh. This is why I couldn't ever be a black witch. I hate spilling blood – mine or others – and I hate being in pain or seeing others in distress. That was why I had healed Fehu; he was in pain and he needed help. Goddess help me if anyone ever learns how soft-hearted I truly am. This realm eats the weak for breakfast.

The hot blood bubbled up and I let it drain into the wooden bowl. When it reached the one-litre mark, I took my paintbrush and quickly painted on *hagalaz* for injury and *sowilo* for health. Thank the Goddess that was over. I was feeling dizzy and my ears were ringing. I powered the painted runes with a little more oomph and the cut on my arm vanished, not even leaving a mark to show where it had been.

I removed the stopper from one of the vials of hydration potion and downed the whole thing in one. It tasted foul but the world stopped swaying, the buzzing in my ears stopped instantly and energy rushed back into my limbs. I got to my feet and rinsed the used vial carefully and placed it in my vial holder to return to the potion store. I pocketed the spare hydration potion; thankfully I wasn't feeling so ill that I needed two. I'd take the spare one back to the potion store later.

I carried the bowl of my blood into the other room where Grimmy seemed to be having a one-sided chat with Fehu. I cleared my throat. 'I'm ready.'

'I reckon you are,' Grimmy drawled. 'Bring the blood over here and pour it on the pentagram.'

'I know what I'm doing,' I huffed.

'Of course you do, bless your heart.' His tone of voice suggested I didn't know anything and I sent him a glare.

He floated up and flicked his pages to the middle. 'You'll be needing to paint these three runes in the middle of the pentagram.'

The three runes he showed me were *angrepet* for attack, *platsar* for location, and *uttrycksyn,* which means 'to show'. These runes aren't part of the sacred twenty-four; they are forbidden ones, dark runes. They aren't taught to good little witches. Though I'm no black witch, I never said I was good.

I poured most of the blood into the pentagram and directed it with my magic to paint on the marks I had already made. I used the remaining blood to paint the three dark runes, then set down my paintbrush and powered them. My eyes clouded over as the vision came to me.

I could see a woman. She was in her human form, and she had dark eyes and hair like her father. She was strapped to a table. Both her and the room were covered in runes. The room had tools and shelves lining the room, a garage perhaps? The vision moved me out of that room and into the kitchen. I saw a green-skinned dryad cooking dinner on the hob whilst making faces at her kids. They were all laughing as if they didn't have a care in the world, let alone a captive in their garage.

The vision pulled back a bit further, showing me the house and then the street name, but I didn't need them. I had recognised the dryad.

Chapter 9

As the spell completed, another bout of dizziness washed over me. Grimmy's payment was being gifted to him and the book glowed golden with the sudden infusion of additional power. Sometimes I got Grimmy out just to chat when the loneliness got too much, but for now I put him back to sleep.

He lives only through the bargains that he makes. He now had six more weeks of time on this earth and I had six weeks less, so I didn't want to waste his time or mine with idle chatter. I wished him goodnight and he called me a peach, then the book landed on the floor, prone and silent. I took him back to my safe and locked him away.

I texted Bastion that I had a location for his daughter. While I waited for his response, I cleaned up the runes in the pentagram and scrubbed the blood from my living-room floor. I laid my rug back down, covering the permanent pentagram hidden underneath it.

Technically, giving up six weeks of your life force in exchange for three dark runes *might* be dark magic. That doesn't make me a black witch – but maybe a grey one. *Don't do what I do, do what I say,* my mum used to say, but she had used the odd dark rune whilst forbidding me to do so. In my view, it's not the forbidden runes that make you a black witch but what you do with them. I had chosen to give my own blood and pain to the spell. I could have killed a chicken or a goat to get the same effect but I had never sacrificed a life or hurt another for a spell, and I didn't intend to start now.

When my apartment was clean and all hints of forbidden magic were gone, I opened all the curtains. Fehu flew to the balcony door and looked at me expectantly. I felt a sting of disappointment that he was leaving me, but of course he had to go back to whomever he was bonded with. I opened the door to let him go but instead he flew back to my shoulder and gave my hair an affectionate nuzzle. I stroked him. 'Come back whenever you like, Fehu. You're welcome here any time.'

'Kraa.' He nuzzled me one last time before taking flight and leaving. He might not be my familiar, but he did like me. Goddess, what a state of affairs that I was happy to have even a *bird* befriend me. Without my book and my bird, I was depressingly alone.

I shut the balcony door and went to my home office in what should have been a second bedroom. I have my main office on the ground floor of the coven building and I try to be seen working there, especially when I've posted my office hours. But when I want to work late, I retreat to my home office where I can work in my pyjamas with no one any the wiser.

I fired up the laptop and checked my emails. Ethan and Jeb had both responded, Jeb with grovelling apologies for the abhorrent state of the potion store and Ethan with a mere acknowledgement of my command. He wouldn't admit any wrongdoing in writing; he was the stubbornest witch I knew – bar myself. Then I pulled up the coven's accounts to review who had been earning what that day.

My ward runes sent a warning, which distracted me from my paperwork. I tried to quash the hope that it was Fehu come for a visit again. I strode into the living room and found my intruder. Bastion was sitting on my chair on my balcony, waiting for me to acknowledge him and let him in.

I checked my phone. No response from him, just his presence on my balcony. Rude bastard.

I crossed the distance between us and opened the sliding door. 'You should have used the ground-floor entrance. It is not acceptable to drop by onto my balcony!'

He ignored my complaint. 'You found my daughter.'

'I did,' I agreed, giving him nothing further.

'Tell me where she is,' he demanded.

'No, not yet. I'll have to come with you to release her. The place is runed to the hilt – and I want you to agree not to harm the kidnapper.'

He fixed his dark eyes on mine. 'And why would I agree to that?' he asked softly, dangerously.

'Because I know her and there are extenuating circumstances.'

'And those are?'

'Your daughter killed her husband.'

'That does not make it acceptable for her to kidnap Charlize.'

I folded my arms. 'From where I'm standing it does.' In the early days after Jake's loss, I had fantasised about having Bastion at my mercy – I had even thought about which runes I could use on him. But fantasies are exactly that. Besides, I hadn't needed to do anything to him because he'd strolled into a black witch's curse. I didn't need to lift a finger. He would die and my hands would be clean.

He raised an eyebrow. 'Did you think of me tied up at your mercy?' His voice was low and seductive.

Ugh. As if. I felt myself flush. 'I don't think of you at all,' I snarled.

'Good. Because just so you know, I prefer to be the one tying the knots.'

My flush deepened. 'I couldn't give a toss about your preferences. Shall we focus on retrieving your daughter?'

He smiled. 'I like seeing you flustered.'

'I'm not flustered – I'm busy. And you're wasting my time. And Charlize's,' I added pointedly.

'Fine. Let's go. I'll shift and you can ride on my back.'

'Absolutely not. I am not now – or ever – riding you,' I spluttered. 'I'll call my driver and meet you in the garage in five minutes.'

'Give me Charlize's location and I'll meet you there,' he suggested guilelessly.

'Do I look stupid?' I shut the balcony door on him before he could respond in the affirmative then rang Oscar and asked him to get the car ready. I picked up my black tote bag and shoved in some potions and paintbrushes that I would need to deal with the runes I'd seen painted on the walls where Charlize was being held. Once the supplies were packed, I headed for the garage.

Bastion was lounging against the car waiting for me. I gestured for him to get in, rattled off the address for Oscar and locked the doors. The griffin looked faintly amused. 'Do you really think that these pathetic locks will contain me?'

He had a point; I didn't doubt that he could rip through the metal doors like they were paper, even with the witch's curse still on him. On a human, the curse would have led to a quick death but on him it seemed to be a mere inconvenience. However, its effect would increase with each passing day and I was looking forward to the day that karma bit this murderer on the ass.

I could wholly relate to Joyce Evergreen's decision to capture her husband's killer but Abigay had been clear: I needed to rescue Charlize to achieve greatness and make a difference in this life. Nothing would stop me on my path to success. Not even Joyce's revenge.

Chapter 10

I turned to Bastion. 'As part of the terms of my assistance, there can be no retribution on the kidnapper from you, from Charlize, from anyone.'

'Agreed,' he muttered grudgingly, jaw tight.

'Good. Then we should discuss the price for my help,' I said as we came to a stop outside of Joyce's house. 'It cost me a great deal to find your daughter.' My life force, to be precise.

'I was under no illusions that you were helping me for free. Everything you do has a price tag.'

That stung a little. He was wrong – I'd healed Fehu because it was the right thing to do and there was no payment involved – but he didn't need to know that. I did not care a whit about his good opinion. I named a price that would make most men blanch but the assassin didn't bat an eyelid.

'Agreed.'

Damn it, I should have asked for more. The truth was, that infusion of cash would keep Mum in her care home for the next year. I might even set aside a little cash of my own for things other than my mum or potion ingredients. I had rented a house for Jake and I for many years and it had been both a relief and a kicker to let it go; it was one less thing to pay for, but my heart ached at the thought of someone else sitting where Jake had sat, someone strolling through the gardens that he had crafted by scent alone.

I glared at Bastion. 'Let's get this over with. I dislike sharing air with you.'

'You dislike sharing. Your mum should have gotten you a pet when you were a child.' That scored a direct hit but, although I hadn't had my own familiar, I'd had Lucille who'd been a kind of pet. But he didn't deserve to know that so I glared some more and said nothing.

We both turned our attention to the house. 'There are kids in there,' I said finally. 'We'll talk our way in. Just stay out of sight for a moment.' His lips tightened but he didn't argue.

'Oscar, you can stay here,' I instructed gently.

'Ma'am ... ' he started to protest. Oscar only calls me ma'am when we have company.

'Stay,' I repeated firmly as I swung myself and my bag out of the car.

Bastion had disappeared by the time I knocked on the door. He couldn't do invisibility like some of the strongest wizards can, so I assumed he was on the roof in his griffin form. I knocked firmly on the door and a beat later it opened.

Joyce gave me a welcoming smile. 'Miss DeLea! How nice to see you!'

'Hi, Joyce. Can I come in? I'd like to check on Wren.'

Joyce's smile dimmed. 'You said there would be no long-lasting effects after the black witch...'

'And there shouldn't be,' I hastened to reassure her. 'I just want to check her over. Can I come in?'

Joyce tossed an uneasy look over her shoulder towards her garage, but in the end her need to make sure her daughter was all right won. She stepped back to let me in then led me to the lounge. Rose was crawling on the floor, knocking over blocks that Wren was stacking for her. 'Hi Wren,' I greeted the little girl.

'Hullo,' she replied, moving closer to her mother. 'You're the witch who helped me.'

'That's right. I'm just here for a check-up, like a dentist or an optician. Can I run a test?' She nodded but pressed closer into her mum's side.

I rarely use my magic without the help of runes or potions because it drains far faster, but Wren had once been covered in black runes and I thought more rune work would be too much for her to bear. Instead, I reached out with my magic and let its warm summer breeze fill me before I drifted it over her.

Her aura was reassuringly clean and clear and I smiled. 'She's absolutely fine.' I gave Wren a thumbs-up. 'Great work.'

Wren sagged into her mum's arms with relief and I let them have a few moments together before I intruded. 'Actually, Joyce, can we have a quick chat about another matter? Let's pop into the kitchen.' This discussion wasn't for children's ears.

Joyce got the hint. 'Wren, keep an eye on Rose for a moment.' She did a quick sweep of the room to check there were no hazards before we left the kids alone.

I followed her into the kitchen and shut the kitchen door behind us. 'You've got a griffin in your garage,' I stated bluntly. 'You have to let her go.'

'Oh, thank God!' Joyce burst out. 'I thought I wanted her to die but then – I couldn't do it. Even though she took Reggie from me and from my girls ... I can't do it.' She wrung her hands. 'But now I've got a bloody griffin in my garage and I don't know what the hell to do with her.'

'I'll take care of her,' I promised.

'And what about retribution? The griffins are going to be so mad at me,' she wailed.

'It was a poor decision, made in grief. I'll make sure there's no blowback.' I'd already made sure of it. 'Take me to the garage and I'll dissipate the runes, then you and I are going to discuss which witch helped you with this.'

'I don't know her name – I never even met her. It was the black witch taking Wren that got me thinking about it. You couldn't find Wren by scrying, so I suddenly realised that I could get someone to do the same for me. I contacted Ronan's associates and they kidnapped Charlize and deposited her here. They had a black witch come and rune the place up. But I have no names of any of those involved. I'm sorry.'

I studied her, but as far as I could see she was telling me the truth. 'I'll need the name of Ronan's associates.'

She bit her lip. 'I'm sorry, but no. I trusted Ronan but his men are dangerous. I can't afford to make enemies of them.'

'But you want to make an enemy of me?' I said, my voice low and threatening.

She smiled gently. 'You act tough, Coven Mother, but I've already seen that your heart is in the right place. You never sent me an invoice for helping Wren. By withholding the names, I'm protecting my family. I think you can respect that.'

Dammit, I did respect it. No need to tell her that I'd sent her portion of the invoice to Lucy because the pack had more than enough funds to pay me, and Joyce had a family to raise. I wasn't going to be responsible for crippling them financially, not when there was another paymaster with deeper pockets. 'Let's go into the garage,' I said instead.

She led me through a door in the kitchen that opened directly into the garage. As she flicked on the lights, a truly impressive display of runes became visible. In the centre of the room, tied to a table, was a young woman with vibrant dark hair and panicked eyes. She had a gag in her mouth. The fear in her eyes made my stomach lurch in sympathy.

'I'm here to help you,' I reassured Charlize. It was hard to reconcile the fact that this girl was a deadly assassin – she only looked to be in her twenties. Griffins are long-lived, though not immortal, so she could have been anything between twenty and two hundred. But I knew for a fact that Bastion was only in his second century, so she couldn't be as old as him.

'Open the garage door to the outside,' I ordered Joyce as I patiently started painting the cancelling rune *ezro* on every rune I could see.

Joyce opened the garage door. She squeaked and froze as Bastion stalked in. He was in his griffin form, his golden eyes burning with fury at the sight of his daughter's incarceration. He let out a shriek and the sound of his rage echoed around the room. Then he stalked towards Joyce.

Uh-oh.

Chapter 11

It looked like Bastion had forgotten his promise to me. I dropped my paintbrush onto the concrete floor and hastily inserted myself between him and Joyce. 'No,' I said firmly. I reached out and tapped him firmly on his beak. 'You promised no retribution. Now shift to human so we can get Charlize out of here.'

He glared at me with golden eyes, so unlike his dark, human ones. His eyes, regardless of their colour, always radiated danger. I held his deadly gaze and lifted my chin stubbornly. He let out another shriek and stretched and flapped his huge wings with enough force to send my red hair billowing back and spilling from its plait.

I didn't flinch. 'Shift,' I demanded again.

There was a beat, then he shimmered and stood on two legs. His dark eyes were no less malevolent than his golden ones had been a beat earlier. 'I may have agreed to no retribution,' he ground out to Joyce, 'but your name will be noted. No griffin will come to your aid. Ever.'

Joyce swallowed and gave a jerky nod of acceptance.

'Go,' I ordered her. 'See to your children.' Before Bastion changed his mind.

Bastion ignored her as she fled and focused on his daughter. He drew a knife from an ankle holster and sliced through the ropes that were binding her to the table. He sat her up and carefully removed her gag. 'Are you hurt?' he asked softly.

She shook her head and licked parched lips. 'No. She didn't hurt me – but she hasn't fed me. She barely gave me anything to drink.' Her voice was dry and rasping.

I grimaced. The hydration potion was burning a hole in my pocket. Why had I taken *two* vials from the potion store? One would surely have been sufficient for me. I don't believe in coincidence; the Goddess had ordered me to find Charlize and then she'd seen fit to encourage me to select two hydration potions.

It stuck in my craw to help Bastion in any way, but his daughter did not deserve to suffer for his sins. No doubt she would have her own to contend with. I opened the vial and passed it to her. 'A hydration potion.'

She flicked her eyes to her father, who nodded that she could trust me, then guzzled it down. 'Oh, thank God,' she murmured when she'd drained the vial. 'I feel so much better. Thank you.'

I nodded tightly and went back to the runes. I hadn't finished cancelling them all before Bastion had clomped in with murder in his eyes. I finished painting *ezro* on them all, then quickly swapped potions and paintbrushes and painted on *pethro*, the revelation rune. A magical signature floated before my eyes.

It was the same signature as that of the witch who had hurt Fehu. In some ways that was a relief because it made it more likely that I was still looking for just one black witch rather than a hidden coven.

'What are you doing?' Bastion's voice was so close it made me jump.

I whirled around. 'None of your business. You have your daughter. Now go.'

'She can't shift. She has runes painted on her. She's weak.'

I sighed, put the revealing potion back in my tote bag and returned to Charlize. She was watching me with impassive eyes; the panic had gone and some of her spirit had returned. Good. I hoped she'd recover from her kidnapping more quickly than I had. Mine still haunted my dreams.

'Remove your shirt, please,' I instructed. She did, but I couldn't see any runes on her skin with my naked eye. I'd seen them in the vision, though, so I knew they were there. The Goddess had guided me, so Charlize must be covered in invisible runes. 'Take off your shoes, please.'

No one ever runes the soles of the feet because there is too high a chance of the runes smearing while they are wet, so there was little chance an invisible rune would be there to interfere with my rune's efficacy. It's my favourite place to paint a *pethro*-revealing rune.

Charlize removed her shoes and socks and showed a foot with a lovely pedicure. I painted *pethro* on her sole and she lit up like a Christmas tree. It was going to take ages to nullify these.

'Bastion, go for a walk. She's going to need to strip completely. The runes are everywhere.'

'I'm not leaving,' he growled. 'I'll wait outside.'

'Fine. Don't come in until I say it's clear,' I ordered. He went, shutting the garage door behind him, giving us some privacy.

Charlize was looking at me with interest. 'I've never seen someone order Dad around before. Well, not do it and live. Even Shirdal asks nicely.'

I ignored that. 'Strip,' I said in a business-like tone.

She removed her clothes. I got some wipes out of my bag and tried to remove the runes but they wouldn't budge; they'd been soaked into her skin for too long.

I started the arduous chore of painting *ezro* on the hundreds of runes on Charlize's skin. Interestingly none of them were dark runes, and I hoped that meant that my black witch was just starting off on his or her path of darkness. Maybe if I found them in time, I could stage an intervention.

Black witch or not, he or she had been incredibly thorough. I found runes to prevent shifting, runes to keep Charlize hidden, runes to remove her supernatural strength – the witch had thought of everything. If they hadn't been there for such a dark purpose, I would have been impressed at the rune combinations.

After an hour of painting, I had neutralised every single one. As I'd worked, tension had increased in Charlize's body until her hands were clenching and unclenching rhythmically. My own hands were cramping from holding the paintbrushes for so long. I was looking forward to a long soak in the tub when I got home.

'All done,' I said abruptly. 'Get dressed.'

'Thank you,' she said tightly.

I ignored her thanks. Her father would pay in spades. As I carefully packed up my supplies, Charlize let her father back in. He pulled her in for a hug. 'All okay?' he asked, scanning her face for any signs of discomfort.

'I'm fine,' she responded. Her voice was stiff and she didn't seem fine to me, but what did I know?

'What were you doing when you got taken?' Bastion asked. 'You didn't have any jobs on – I checked with Shirdal when I was trying to track you.'

Charlize flushed. 'I took a job off the books. Obviously it was a setup.'

'When will you learn?' he growled. 'It was an off-the-books job that got you into this mess in the first place! Shirdal vets every job. You can't just take any old job just because you don't want the guild to take its cut!'

'The guild is bullshit! Shirdal keeps giving me shit jobs! He's still punishing me.'

'You knew there would be a consequence to the tourneys and you did them anyway. You reap what you sow, Charlize. No more off-the-books work. If I hear of you taking any unsanctioned work, I'll take you back to Alamut myself,' he threatened.

She swallowed hard.

'Do you hear me young lady?' he demanded. Charlize nodded. 'This is the last straw, Charlize.

I'm serious. Shirdal thought you were ready, but if you keep pulling stunts like this then you're not.'

'I am!' she insisted. 'I am. I won't do it again, I swear. I promise, Dad. I just wanted to prove myself.'

Bastion's eyes softened and he tucked her hair behind her ear. 'You have nothing to prove.' He rested his hand on her shoulder and she folded into him. I felt awkward observing such a personal moment between them. Even I had to admit he was a good father.

He drew back to look at her, noting the tension in her frame. 'When did you last kill?' He asked the question like other people would ask when you'd last eaten. For the griffins, it was just as necessary.

She grimaced. 'Too long ago.' Her voice broke and a stray tear slid down her cheek. 'Dad, it's tearing at me.' She started to sob.

He wrapped an arm around her, pulled out his phone and speed dialled. 'I have an emergency. Do you have anything for me?' He listened for a beat. 'I'll take it.' He hung up and turned to Charlize. 'Let's go.' They walked out without a backward glance at me.

'You're welcome,' I huffed into the silence. That griffin had no manners.

Chapter 12

I informed Joyce that her garage no longer had active runes or an occupant, then gave her plenty of dire warnings about what would happen to her if she ever did anything so mule-headed again. I promised that this time I would leave the Connection out of the whole sordid affair but next time, if there *was* a next time, I'd bring down the full force of the law on her. Threats duly dispensed, I headed back to the car.

'Everything okay, Am?' Oscar asked as I slid into the passenger seat beside him. When I rode in the front of the car, it was because I needed his steadying presence.

I undid my ruined braid, let my hair flow over my shoulders and massaged the tight feeling at the base of my skull. 'It's been a long day.' I sighed. 'How did Ethan and Jeb get on sorting out the potion store?'

He flashed me a grin. 'Ethan was spitting fury. He's embarrassed.'

'So he should be! *I'm* embarrassed. What if the triune had checked in there? I would never have lived it down.'

'He was still sorting it when I left. It'll be perfectly organised – if not restocked – by the end of the day.'

I pressed my lips together. 'I should have done a spot check earlier.'

'We're all fallible, Am. Cut yourself some slack – you can't be everywhere at once. You run yourself ragged for the coven. All those extra jobs you take outside of working hours to fill the coven's coffers? Don't think the others don't notice because they do. They're in awe of you.'

Slightly mollified, I closed my eyes and lay my head against the headrest. 'I'm sorry Mum didn't remember you today.'

He sighed softly. 'Me too.' He gave my hand a brief squeeze before returning it to the wheel.

'I miss her,' I admitted. It was easier to say things like that with my eyes closed.

'Me too,' he murmured again. 'She was, and is, very proud of you. So am I, kiddo.' The old nickname made me smile, despite the fact that it was a wildly inaccurate term of endearment these days.

'Thanks.' Silence stretched out for a minute or two before I broke it. 'We have a black witch amongst us.'

'Indeed,' he agreed with a sigh.

I was glad Oscar had reached the same conclusion, though I wished it wasn't true. The rest of the journey passed in silence. We said goodnight perfunctorily; we're not a big huggy-kissy family and Oscar is undoubtedly family. He is the father I should have had. I had spent many a teenage year wishing he could be my blood before finally realising it didn't matter a damn that he wasn't.

I went up to my flat. I couldn't decide if I wanted to sleep or have a bath, but the twinges in my hands decided for me. I ran a hot bath with plenty of lavender and a dash of another potion of my own invention. I call it 'aches away' because that's what it does and I am imaginative like that. The bath was still running when there was a knock at my door.

'Just a minute!' It took me a moment to pull on a bathrobe but when I went to get the door, I saw that someone had already popped in. Oscar: no one else was keyed to my rune wards. On my dining-room table sat a champagne flute of fizz. I smiled; it was exactly what I needed to wash away the day.

'Thank you,' I called, but he had already gone. I grabbed the Champagne and took it with me to the bath, along with a trashy romance novel that I would deny reading until the day that I died. I climbed into the hot water and let out a soft gasp as the warmth penetrated my aching limbs.

I took a big pull of Champagne and let the bubbles burst on my tongue, then dried my hands on the towel hanging close by and picked up the novel. It had a man-chest cover on it that I took a moment to admire; I do so love muscles. This was a tale about a rich princess being captured by a pirate for ransom. I was just getting to the bodice-ripping bit and feeling thoroughly relaxed when my wards flared red again. Son of a—

I climbed out of the bath feeling the much-needed relaxation drain away. Still wet, I hastily pulled my bathrobe back on and took the book and empty glass to the kitchen sink. Then I marched to my balcony to glare at its occupant.

I flung open the door. 'What did I say?' I snarled. 'If you must keep visiting me, do it through the proper channels!'

Bastion looked amused and his eyes flickered down to the soapsuds clinging to my legs. I resisted the urge to tie my bathrobe more tightly.

He held out a briefcase. 'What is that?' I demanded.

'Payment.'

I took the heavy briefcase from him and lugged it inside. He followed me in, his eagle eyes missing nothing – including the well-thumbed novel resting by the sink. He smirked as his eyes fell on the cover and I fought the blush that wanted to rise up my cheeks. It was none of his damned business what I read.

'What's the code?' I snarled.

'Zero zero zero zero.'

'Very inventive,' I said sarcastically. I put in the number, clicked open the locks – and saw more cash than I'd ever seen before. 'Most people do bank transfers,' I muttered.

'As an assassin, people tend to prefer to pay me in cash.' He shrugged. 'I had it on hand.'

Of course he did. How rich was he? I sat at my table, pulled out the bank notes and started counting them suspiciously.

Bastion looked amused at my distrust. 'Can I get a cup of tea while you count it all?' he asked.

I glared but grudgingly stood up to make him one. Mum had instilled manners into me, unlike Bastion's mother who had obviously failed to train her son. Besides, I could do with a cup of tea myself. I always like a cup of tea before bed. I busied myself pulling out mugs and filling the kettle. I smirked a little as I gave his mug a wash, I would enjoy watching him drink out of a mug which said *I could agree with you, but then we'd both be wrong.*

Bastion watched me smirk with narrowed eyes. 'Are you going to spit in my tea?'

'Not while you're watching,' I responded sweetly. 'But if you're hankering after a sub-standard brew, we can skip boiling the water.'

'No, that's okay. Though if you put the milk in first, I'm not drinking it.'

I rolled my eyes. 'Obviously. I'm not a barbarian.' I plonked a mug ungraciously in front of him. I sipped from my own mug, which read *An educated woman is to be feared.* Damn right.

Bastion picked up the mug. 'Thank you.' His lips twitched as he read the brusque mug. Darn, I'd wanted to annoy him.

'So you do have *some* manners,' I snapped.

'More than you.'

I folded my arms. 'What's that supposed to mean?'

He sipped his tea and looked at me over his cup of nectar from the gods. 'You're condemning me to death. It doesn't seem very polite.'

'I have nothing to do with your death. A black witch cursed you. Your death will lie at her door, not mine,' I said firmly.

'Sophistry, witch. You could save me and you choose not to.'

I sipped my brew and carried on counting. 'It's all there,' I noted finally. 'Now leave. Our business is over.'

Bastion stood. He set his mug of tea beside the sink before he casually sauntered to the balcony and slid open the door. He climbed onto the balcony's metal frame, his legs dangling seven floors above the ground, turned back to me and sent me an indecipherable look. 'Amber DeLea ... our business is far from over.'

Then he leapt from my balcony, shimmering as he fell into his griffin form. I watched his wings beat the air as he flew away.

I couldn't decide if his final words to me were a threat ... or a promise.

Keep reading to enjoy a sneak peek of Chapter One of Hex of the Witch!

What's Next?

I hope you've enjoyed Amber's prequel novella! Next up in this witchy saga is Hex of the Witch! Once more Amber has to work with Bastion, and she is *not* happy about it...

In the meantime, if you'd like FREE BOOKS then join my newsletter and you can get a couple of free stories, as well as pictures of my dog and other helpful things.

Patreon

I have started my very own Patreon page. What is Patreon? It's a subscription service that allows you to support me AND read my books way before anyone else! For a small monthly fee you could be reading my next book, on a weekly chapter-by-chapter basis (in its roughest draft form!) in the next week or two. If you hit "Join the community" you can follow me along for free, though you won't get access to all the good stuff, like early release books, polls, live Q&A's, character art and more! You can even have a video call with me or have a character named after you! My current patrons are getting to read a novella called House Bound which isn't available anywhere else, not even to my newsletter subscribers!

If you're too impatient to wait until my next release, then Patreon is made for you! Join my patrons here.

Stay in Touch

I have been working hard on a bunch of cool things, including a new and shiny website which you'll love. Check it out at www.heathergharris.com.

If you want to hear about all my latest releases – subscribe to my newsletter for news, fun and freebies. Subscribe at my website www.heathergharris.com/subscribe.

Please note that all of Heather's works are written in British English with British phrases, spellings and grammar being utilised throughout. If you think you have found a typo, please do let Heather know at heathergharrisauthor@gmail.com

Sneak Peak

Read on for a sneak peak of *Hex of the Witch!*

Hex of the Witch - Chapter 1

The building was on fire. Again. I pinched the bridge of my nose and turned to one of the witches who was standing next to me and wringing her hands. 'Tell me you didn't forget to cover your crystal ball.'

Sarah's lip wobbled. 'I'm so sorry, Coven Mother.'

I kept my face carefully neutral, trying to bank my frustration. 'Until you can learn proper potion and crystal-ball care, I'm demoting you to acolyte.'

I resisted the urge to apologise but this wasn't Sarah's first mistake, not by a long shot. And her mistakes were *costly*. She needed supervision and her bruised ego would just have to take the hit.

Sarah wailed at my judgement and collapsed sobbing into the arms of her waiting friends. Ria sent me her best death glare, which I blithely ignored. I contemplated giving Sarah a sympathetic little pat on the arm, but I'd just relegated her back to the ranks of a lowly acolyte so I doubted any comforting gestures from me would be welcome.

I turned back to the newly refurbished building and grimaced at the flames licking at the freshly painted walls.

I hauled out my phone and speed-dialled Dick Symes: Dick by name, dick by nature. Still, the water elemental was local, and one of his extended family would be able to get here faster than the emergency services. No doubt the location of the training house so close to one of the most prestigious water elemental families in the UK was not a simple coincidence but a matter of design by some clever former Coven Mother. Goddess knows, we had needed the elementals often enough lately. The thought made me narrow my eyes again at Sarah.

The phone continued to ring and I struggled to push down my impatience. I didn't need a water elemental in ten minutes, I needed one *now*. Luckily Dick chose that moment to answer. 'Amber DeLea, what do you need?' he asked brusquely.

I appreciated that he got straight to the point. We weren't friends and we didn't need to discuss the weather. 'I need someone to put out a fire at the coven's training house.'

There was a beat of silence. 'Again?'

I couldn't suppress the sigh that slipped out. 'Yes.'

He snickered: *dick*. 'Martin will be with you shortly. It'll cost more this time,' he warned.

I expected nothing less. Nothing is free in the Other realm. 'What do you want?' I asked suspiciously.

'A favour,' he suggested lightly, like it was no big deal.

I wasn't born yesterday. No way was I agreeing to that; it was far too open-ended. 'One favour, to be called in within three months' time. No injury, harm or death to befall anyone as a direct consequence of that favour,' I counter-offered.

'Done,' he agreed triumphantly.

'So mote it be,' I muttered. He sounded entirely too happy for my liking and I hated feeling like I'd got the bad end of a deal.

Dick hung up without another word, and Martin Symes arrived moments later, panting. He'd clearly run from his house – the Symes were *very* local. 'Where do you want me, Miss DeLea?' he asked between pants.

I gestured to the fire behind me, managing to suppress the snarky comment that wanted to slip out. I deserved a medal for my self-control.

'Right you are!' He strode towards the house and seconds later water was pouring from his fingers into the training house. I winced at the damage the torrent was causing, but it put out the fire and that had been the more immediate problem.

'Thank you, Martin. Now can you remove the excess water from the scene?' That was one of the main advantages to using a water elemental instead of the fire department: Martin could soak up all the excess water like a dry sponge. It helped minimise the water damage on top of the fire damage.

He nodded enthusiastically and struck a suitably dashing pose whilst he drew the water back into himself. It would have looked more dashing if he hadn't kept looking over his shoulder to make sure the gaggle of young witches were still watching him.

I called Jeb, the witch who was responsible for coven maintenance. 'Coven Mother, how can I help?' he answered warmly.

'There's been another fire at the training house,' I said, trying to keep my voice even.

'No!' he protested. 'The refurbishment was finished literally yesterday,' he whined, his tone disbelieving.

'Believe me, I know.' Jeb may have organised the work but I'd paid for it. 'You'll need to get to the site to assess the damage.'

'Who was it this time?'

'Sarah Bellington.'

'Again?'

'Indeed. She's been demoted to acolyte.'

He whistled. 'Rightly so, but Venice is going to be so pissed off.' Sarah's mum was a force to be reckoned with – but so am I.

'Goodness that was close. I almost gave a damn,' I snarked back. 'Sarah left her crystal ball uncovered.'

'Oh for fuck's sake,' Jeb cursed loudly. I didn't swear aloud but I wholeheartedly agreed with the sentiment. He cleared his throat. 'Whilst we're sharing bad news, the Crone has returned.'

I frowned. 'What do you mean, she's returned?' The Triune – the Maiden, the Mother and the Crone – had only left that morning after visiting us for three long weeks. Three weeks of seeing to their every need. I'm not used to bowing and scraping – it's not in my skillset – but the Holy Triune demand my respect and, to a degree, my subservience.

It was galling. Of course, I love the Crone herself – Aunt Abigay is one of my mum's best friends and she had helped raise me after my father abandoned us – but our relationship has changed over the years. As the Crone, she holds a sacred, lifelong position in witch society. The Crone is considered to have one of the highest positions in the coven; a position that doesn't allow much room for favouritism or nepotism, more's the pity.

The Triune had left our tower this morning and were supposed to be returning to the coven council in Edinburgh. 'She's back,' Jeb reiterated. 'She requests an audience with you at your earliest convenience.'

'Tell her I'm on my way. You'll have to deal with the situation here.'

'I'm on it, Coven Mother,' Jeb promised.

We hung up and I strode to my waiting car. As I slid into the back seat, I met Oscar's blue eyes in the rear-view mirror. 'Back to the coven, please,' I instructed. I didn't look back at the desolate scene behind me, weeks of work all gone up in smoke because of one idiot's thoughtlessness. Covering your crystal ball is Basic Witchery 101. Sarah was making me look bad and I couldn't afford that – not now.

I wanted to be the witch member for the Symposium. The Symposium runs the Connection, the governing body for all supernatural beings that exist in the Other Realm. There had been a power vacuum ever since Sky, the last witch Symposium member, had been killed.

The coven council was moving excruciatingly slowly in appointing the new member. In the meantime, its members took turns attending the Symposium meetings. I suspected that they all liked the extra taste of power and weren't in a hurry to relinquish it.

I wanted to be on the Symposium – heck, I wanted to rule it – but one thing at a time. I wanted to craft the change that the Connection so desperately needed, and I wanted to do it from within. Sarah's little stunt made me look bad; if I couldn't handle my own coven, how could I be responsible for all the covens in the country? But the fire had only just happened, so that couldn't possibly be what the Crone wanted with me, could it?

My driver sensed my foul mood so he didn't try for chitchat. Oscar is more than a driver and bodyguard to me – he's been my mother's partner for many years. They'd never formalised their union and now, with Mum's dementia, the opportunity had passed. But Oscar is the father I'd never had after mine skipped out on Mum and me when I was six years old. I was glad she had found happiness in Oscar's arms and only a smidgen jealous that such love had been denied to me.

We pulled up to the coven tower. In the old days, covens lived together in villages but we have modernised our living practices to adapt to modern life and now the covens own their apartment blocks. At the top of mine is a rarely used guest suite that The Crone had been occupying for the last few weeks. No doubt she'd be waiting for me there.

I took the stairs. At forty-two years of age, I need to make the effort to incorporate exercise into my day or the pounds will pile on – especially as I have a weakness for blueberry muffins. When I reached the guest suite, I knocked once on the door.

'Come in,' the Crone called.

She was sitting in a high wingback chair, white afro resting languidly against the purple fabric. She sat up as I walked in and met my eyes. Her dark skin bore a few lines of age but not as many as she was due.

I knew I was in trouble because her pink lipstick-painted lips didn't curve into a smile and her eyes were cold. 'Aunt Abigay—' I started.

She looked at me with a hint of censure. I wasn't her family to be gifted her name now that she was the Crone. 'Coven Mother,' she responded sharply. 'You've been keeping secrets.'

Delve into the rest of Hex of the Witch, coming 19th September 2023.

Other Titles

Heather G. Harris' Other works:-

The Other Realm

0.5. Glimmer of Dragons, a prequel novella,

    1. Glimmer of The Other,

    2. Glimmer of Hope,

    3. Glimmer of Christmas (book 2.5, a Christmas novella)

    4. Glimmer of Death,

5. Glimmer of Deception,

6. Challenge of the Court,

7. Betrayal of the Court; and

8. Revival of the Court.

The Other Wolf

0.5 Defender of The Pack, a prequel novella,
   1. Protection of the Pack,

   2. Guardians of the Pack; and

   3. Saviour of The Pack.

The Other Witch

0.5 Rune of the Witch, a prequel novella,
   1. Hex of the Witch,

   2. Coven of the Witch;,

3. Familiar of the Witch and

4. Destiny of the Witch.

About Heather

Heather is an urban fantasy writer and mum. She was born and raised near Windsor, which gave her the misguided impression that she was close to royalty in some way. She is not, though she once got a letter from Queen Elizabeth II's lady-in-waiting.

Heather went to university in Liverpool, where she took up skydiving and met her future husband. When she's not running around after her children, she's plotting her next book and daydreaming about vampires, dragons and kick-ass heroines.

Heather is a book lover who grew up reading Brian Jacques and Anne McCaffrey. She loves to travel and once spent a month in Thailand. She vows to return.

Want to learn more about Heather? Subscribe to her newsletter for behind-the-scenes scoops, free bonus material and a cheeky peek into her world.

Her subscribers will always get the heads up about the best deals on her books.

Subscribe to her Newsletter at her website www.heathergharris.com/subscribe.

Too impatient to wait for September for Heather's next book? Join her (very small!) army of supportive patrons at Patreon.

Contact Info: www.heathergharris.com

Email: HeatherGHarrisAuthor@gmail.com

Social Media

Heather can also be found on a host of social medias:

Facebook Page

Facebook Reader Group

Goodreads

Bookbub

Instagram

Reviews

Reviews feed Heather's soul. She'd really appreciate it if you could take a few moments to review her books on Amazon,

Bookbub, or Goodreads and say hello.

Printed in Great Britain
by Amazon

41296538R00088